Shearing Time

Allison Paterson
Illustrator Shane McGrath

For Mum and Dad and those who came before. AP

BIG SKY PUBLISHING

First published 2017

Big Sky Publishing Pty Ltd
PO Box 303, Newport, NSW 2106, Australia
Phone: 1300 364 611
Fax: (61 2) 9918 2396
Email: info@bigskypublishing.com.au
Web: www.bigskypublishing.com.au
Typesetting: Think Productions
Printed by Jilin-GIGO International
National Library of Australia Cataloguing-in-Publication entry (pbk and hbk)
Author: Allison Paterson
Title: Shearing Time
ISBN: 978-1-925520-08-8 (hardback)
ISBN: 978-1-925520-09-5 (paperback)

I love shearing time!
It's the best time of the year.

It's school holidays, the frosts have gone
and the paddocks are grassy green.

There are lots of jobs to do.
Mustering the sheep is my favourite.

We **zoom** across the paddocks on
our motorbikes with the dogs chasing
behind – they puff like crazy!

Sometimes they even catch a lift!

The clever dogs crouch down low and
dash about as they round up the sheep.

Grandpa trained them so well that we don't say a word.
Our four-legged friends know just what to do.

We herd the mob back to the shearing shed and settle them safely into the dusty, rowdy yards.

The cranky ewes complain as we draft them from their lambs. Only the mums are having a haircut today.

The shearing team arrives bright and early.

Years ago they camped in the old farmhouse,
but that was when they came by horse and cart.

The shearers wear singlets and grubby jeans.
They're ready for a long, hard day!

When we aren't rounding
up a mob of woolly sheep
we help in the shed.

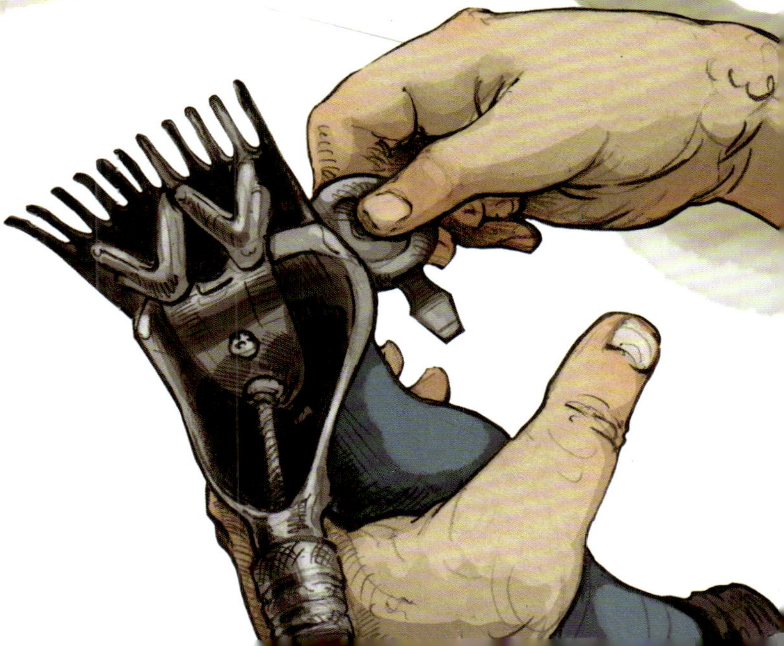

The machines whirr and the sheep are bleating.
The shed **rumbles** with the **racket!**

MACCA

The shorn sheep are pushed down a slippery chute into the outside pens.

We sometimes slide down there too!

No time to rest!

The shearers stretch their backs and drag the next sheep from the catching pen and across the board.

The pens have greasy wooden grating for the floor so the sheep droppings fall to the ground beneath.

When I was little I was scared of falling through the gaps into the stinky sludge.

Yuck!

Dad picks up the fleece, throws it on the sorting table and tears off the dirty bits of wool. That's called skirting. He decides if the grade of the wool is coarse or fine. Fine wool is the best!

After that the sorted fleeces are baled up into wool packs and stamped with our farm's special label.

XBAA

Baling is the **best!**

I clamber into the wool press, sink into the softness of the fleeces, grip the greasy sides and start the stomping.

I am floating on a cloud ... until the prickles stab me!

Ouch!

Then we race home because
it's time for morning tea.

We flip the little pancakes called **drop scones**
while Granny bakes real scones.

Mum carries the boiling hot billy of super strong tea to the shed.

We carry the freshly-baked food and chipped cups in baskets.

Dad makes us go home to eat our morning tea. He doesn't want us to hear any bad words, but we hear them anyway!

Then we all get back to work until lunchtime.

The shearers traipse up the track
and sit around our big kitchen table.

Granny tells them to **mind their manners!**

There is roast lamb, green veges from the garden and piles of crunchy potatoes.

The chocolate pudding for dessert is **delicious!**

The shearers moan that they can't bend over …

I'm sure they really don't mind!

Cleaning up is **not** fun!
I can't wait to head back to the shed.

Mum arrives in the ute to help drove the shorn sheep to their paddock.

On the way back we pick up a load of hay for the bellowing cattle.

The sun is low in the sky as we wander home
with the dogs hovering at our heels …

I wish Grandpa was with us, he would say,

We've done a good day's work!

But Dad remembers and says it instead …

Mum says we smell like sheep and our clothes are
so **dirty** they could stand up by themselves!

I fall into bed extra early. There's no need to count sheep tonight.

As the sun peeks over the horizon we are ready to start the working day all over again ...

I love shearing time!